Hiroshima is synonymous with the first hostile use of an atomic bomb. Many people think of this occurrence as one terrible event in the past, which is studied from history books.

MURAI Shimako and other 'Women of Hiroshima' believe otherwise: for them, the bomb had after-effects which affected countless people for decades, effects that were all the more menacing for their unpredictability – and often, invisibility.

This is a tale of two such people: on the surface successful modern women, yet each bearing underneath hidden scars as horrific as the keloids that disfigured Hibakusha on the days following the bomb.

Shimako Murai

SUNFLOWERS

= LE SOLEIL =

A play in one act

Translated from the Japanese by Ben Jones

Sunflowers – Le Soleil

by Shimako Murai
translated by Ben Jones

For performance rights please contact the publisher.

Published by Ōzaru Books, an imprint of BJ Translations Ltd
Street Acre, St Nicholas-at-Wade, BIRCHINGTON, CT7 0NG, U.K.
https://ozaru.net/ozarubooks

This edition published 6 August 2010 (with minor revisions in 2023)
ISBN: 978-0-9559219-3-3

Translator's introduction

I first visited Hiroshima when hitchhiking through Japan as a young student. The vehicle that gave me a lift into the city from the motorway was – unusually – a taxi, and as normal I engaged the middle-aged driver in casual chat. However, the second he responded 'Yes, I've lived in Hiroshima all my life', I knew that he must have been here on *that day*, and I found myself tongue-tied. Should I ask him 'what was it like?', should I apologize for what 'we Caucasians' had done, should I point out that I wasn't American and hence not really to blame… all sorts of clumsy, naïve thoughts tumbled through my mind. Thankfully he steered the conversation to other topics.

It was the following year that I met Murai *Sensei*, who immediately started telling me the story of Hiroshima I had wanted to hear. It was her own story, indeed the story of her life, and at the same time the story of countless other 'Women of Hiroshima'. She also introduced me to several of these women, often on a purely social level. One in particular struck me as a pleasant, cheerful young business lady – obviously too young to have been affected by the bomb even inside the womb. Yet people say that in Japan the truth is sometimes hidden behind a veil, and it was only much later that the tragic background to this individual's life was revealed. Her story – the difference between the bright exterior and the shaded interior – affected me more than anything else I have read about Hiroshima, and I felt quite privileged to help Murai *Sensei* produce a play in which certain parts were based on her unique history. 'Sunflowers' is of course this story.

I also attempted a first English translation at that time, as Murai *Sensei* stressed that the greatest fear of herself and many other Women of Hiroshima was that their experiences would not be passed on to future generations, either within Japan or abroad. I did however encounter a somewhat bizarre problem in that I felt many of the words and expressions used in Japanese to have a visceral impact which I was unable to recreate in English. Revisiting the translation twenty years later I still find this to be a problem; nevertheless, I hope the story will speak for itself.

The play was first performed in Japanese at Tokyo's Space Zero (October 1989) and Hiroshima's Higashi Ward Civic Arts Center (November 1989), with MAHO Shibuki and TAKAJŌ Miki in the rôles of Kazuko and Hiroko. It was also performed in Czech (translated by Vladimír Procházka) as "Slunečnice" at Činoherní Klub in Prague (April 1992) with Lenka Skopalová and Lucie Trmíková.

The Japanese text was included in the magazine 悲劇喜劇 published by 早川書房 (1 January 1990) and later made available as 向日葵 LE・SOLEIL in 広島の女・八月六日, pub. 影書房 (6 August 1992) ISBN 978-4877140625. The two versions are slightly different, and differ again from the script we used in 1989, so this translation is based on a combination and adaptation of all three. The opening quotation from Rilke was translated directly from the Japanese included in Murai *Sensei*'s text, rather than using one of the existing English translations of "Die Schwestern" or translating anew from the German, but readers may find it interesting to compare them.

The Japanese text also includes a footnote about "moral adoption", explaining that this was a programme initiated via the New York "Saturday Review" in 1949, by the American author Norman Cousins and TANIMOTO Kiyoshi, pastor of Hiroshima's Nagarekawa Church, to look after children orphaned through the atomic bombing.

About the author

MURAI Shimako was born in Hiroshima in 1928. After attending the local Prefectural Girls' School and graduating from Tokyo Woman's Christian University, she was one of the first students to join the Stage Arts Academy (Butai Geijutsu Gakuin) in Tokyo, and continued to study for many years with Yoshi Hijikata, founder of the Shingeki movement. She later went on to Charles University in Prague, where in 1967 she obtained a PhD in Theatrical Science, while working with Czech National Theatre.

In addition to numerous works published as playwright and author, she was the first to translate several Czech works into Japanese, including operas by Janáček and Smetana and plays by Havel, Kundera and Topol. As director, she collaborated with dramatist BETSUYAKU Minoru for over two decades in the group "Katatsumuri no Kai".

She won numerous awards, including the "Kinokuniya Theatre Award" (1968) for translating and directing "Kočka na kolejích" (Cat on the Rails) and "Slavík k večeři" (Nightingale for Dinner) by Josef Topol; an award from the Agency for Cultural Affairs in the National Arts Festival (1985), for her production of her own "Woman of Hiroshima" trilogy; the "Maui Peace Award" (1986) at Maui Hiroshima Day; a "Fringe First Award" (1988) for the English version of "Woman of Hiroshima Part 3 – A Shower of Leaflets" at the Edinburgh Festival; and the Kiyoshi Tanimoto Peace Prize (1997).

Parts of the Woman of Hiroshima series have been performed in English in Maui (1986), Tokyo/Hiroshima (1987) and Edinburgh (1988); in German in Berlin (1988); and in French in Avignon (1989) and Geneva (1990). "Ano hi, ano ame" has been performed in Czech in Prague (1990).

Part 2 of Woman of Hiroshima was published in German as "Eine Frau aus Hiroshima", in "An jenem Tag: literarische Zeugnisse über Hiroshima und Nagasaki", ed. Jürgen Berndt, pub. Verlag Volk und Welt, Berlin, 1986. The entire trilogy was published in Czech (translated by Jan Válek) as Hirošimská Žena, pub. Dilia, 1987. Various other translations (in English, French, Spanish and Russian) are awaiting publication.

Outside her literary activities, Murai worked on Hiroshima City's committee to have the Atomic Bomb Dome designated a World Heritage Site (1994-1996), and was for many years a director of the Japan-Czech Association, as well as teaching at Tokyo College of Photography, and participating in the Japan PEN Club and the Japan Directors Association.

She died in May 2018, at her home in Shinjuku.

Look!

Two people experience and interpret the same happening in quite distinct ways

It is as though different flows of time are cutting through two identical rooms

Rainer Maria Rilke

Dramatis Personæ:

Kazuko (a woman, age 49)

Hiroko (a woman, age 31)

Setting:

Hiroko's restaurant/bar, "Le Soleil" in
Tokyo's bayside warehouse area

Overture: the stage and audience are shrouded in complete darkness

✿ ✿ ✿

Prologue

A single spotlight shines out into the pitch blackness. A woman dressed in an anti-air raid hood and mompe[1] is crouching down, clutching something in both arms as if protecting it. A tableau of a mother hugging her baby.

Suddenly a flash of light, deafening roar, and simultaneously the woman's scream: "Tōru…"

Lighting changes. We see Tōru and Hiroko dancing a tango, many years ago.

✿ ✿ ✿

Lighting changes. A bright room, with an antique bust on a stand near the front, and a modern bicycle near the back.

(Enter young woman, dressed in Capri pants and white T-shirt, combing her hair)

HIROKO: Oh shit, why does it have to be today? Should I just wear the same clothes as usual, or would something else look better? Calm

____

[1] *Loose pantaloons with a "splashed" pattern, commonly (later compulsorily) worn as working clothes by Japanese women in WW2*

down Hiroko, there's no need to panic… But the phone call last night was a bit strange, not like Kazuko normally is: "I'm flying out from Narita Airport tomorrow, so I wondered if we could meet up quickly beforehand…" It's all very well to say "quickly" but we both know that it makes no difference how long we talk. Every time we meet, it's always the same: "You're still young, why don't you reconsider…?" – that's all she ever says.

(Whistle of kettle boiling)

Buggeration, now the kettle's boiling over, what on earth am I doing? That's why I told her I'd prefer to meet somewhere else…

(Exit. Re-enters with hair in ponytail)

I just can't relax, something never feels quite right. I end up losing track of where I am and what I'm doing.

(Goes to bicycle at back of room, holds handlebar in a daydream.)

Tōru, you were always very concerned about my cycling. I never quite understood why. Whenever I went anywhere on the bike, you'd say "Remember, go slowly now!" and give me a pat on the back… you never rode one yourself. Well of course you had a car, didn't you, your van. Always using it to carry somebody or something around…

(Puts on a cassette tape of music)

"Hey Onīsan, why is it always this song you play?" But you'd just look into the rear-view mirror and smile. "Could you stop calling me Onīsan?" That was another thing you asked me in the van. You were so kind to

everyone – that's why I started calling you Onīsan, elder brother, because I felt that if you thought of me as your little sister, you might treat
me as someone more special. "Why, does it annoy your sister? Does she
say things like 'Not another younger sister? Aren't the two of us
enough?' or something?" You burst out laughing, and just said "Don't
worry about Kazuko!", nothing more. "No Tōru, I can't stand it, I really
can't! If there's something you want to say, then go ahead and say it!"

(Stops tape)

"Marry me!"

That was just after my Coming of Age ceremony, so I must have been
20 years old. It was like "Smack!" being hit in the head by a football. I
was living a pretty carefree life, and certainly had no thoughts of marriage or the like. I was an only child, and just wanted some friends. I
was always hanging onto someone. I looked up to you so much.

(Rings bicycle bell)

You seemed to be able to do absolutely anything – everyone said so.

(Heaves the bicycle up onto its back wheel, stands holding it)

"That man is really a vet. But now he's become a builder, putting up
houses, doing the internal decorations, even creating beautiful furniture… a bit old, mind you, but still…"

(Spins front wheel)

'The tall old guy' – I thought the same way at first, but gradually I came
to think of you as my elder brother. Oh that's right, after that one day…

My little Pépé had fallen sick, so I phoned you up – but you hurriedly gave me the name of a friend's clinic. "Couldn't you have a look at him yourself?" I asked, but you replied "I gave up my practice, and there's no turning back. I've had my fill of working with life and death problems. So hurry up, get Pépé to the clinic quickly!" Once Pépé was better, I brought him round to show you, and you picked him up and hugged him, saying "Take care of yourself, little one!" Then you gave him a kiss. That was the first time I saw you kiss. "Ooh Pépé, you got a kiss – aren't you the lucky one!" The moment I said that, you went deep crimson and handed Pépé back to me. I could never think of you as 'the old guy' any more after that.

(Lays bicycle down on ground)

I was helping my mother in her antique shop. My main job was simply watching over the shop, with the additional responsibility of interpreting for her occasional foreign customers: "May-I-help-you?" "Unless you've got something against it, Hiroko, I'll speak to your mother!" I fainted in your van, and you scooped me up in your arms and took me home to Mum… then asked her permission, and even said, "You could come to live with us too, Mum!"

(Puts tape back on. Exit. Re-enters in smart dress and high heels)

It seems like just a dream now… It was all over so quickly, wasn't it? I moved in to your flat immediately, leaving Pépé at my mother's. Mum was just gone 40, and quite strong-willed… "You must be joking, me come and live with a newly-wed couple?!" Her marriage had ended in divorce, and she hated formal ceremonies. "I think you should just do exactly what you want… provided of course you let all your friends know". Well that alone took us two weeks, because we both had so many friends. Your friends tended to made a joke of it, saying "What, you mean you're serious this time?"

Maybe that's really how it looked then, because we only got… coupled… later. "I'm not Pépé! I want to be kissed much, much more!" – that's how I teased you after the party broke up. You don't touch alcohol, so it was only me who drank with the guests. Quite a lot had come, because everyone knew you were a good cook. My friends all praised your cooking, and told me how jealous they were. Even Mum said "How lovely it is to be able to relax and have a good time for once, without having to worry about the food!" But I prefer your kisses to your cooking. So sweet…! That very first day, you told me, "You greet me as though embracing the sunlight…"

(Lost in memories)

I never wanted to be apart from you, not for a moment. I wanted everything to stay just as it was forever. I even hated unlacing my arms from your back. Who could have imagined that such happiness could exist in this world… You were bright and cheerful, your shoulders looked sturdy enough to take me on a flight to absolutely anywhere…

Hey, do you remember the cake your friend from the French pâtisserie made for us? Wasn't it fantastic, a square white cake just like a miniature of the room where you and I lived. Remember? The day it came, some pigeons were cooing outside our bedroom window. "Coo, coo" – the two of them were chattering away. "Do you think they know that there are two of us in here now, too?" You got out of bed, and watched the pigeons through the white lace curtains… Seeing your bare back so far away, I somehow felt lonely… "Tōru, come back to me, please?" As you turned back towards me, your smiling face looked like a bashful schoolboy. With the light behind you, it was as though I was looking at a film negative. You drew in your chin a bit, walked over to me and asked, "Do you like white doves?" "Yes, I suppose they're quite pretty." I ran my fingers through your hair and kissed your forehead. "I prefer ones which are like the two out there – the kind you find everywhere, grey with a touch of green or white. It's always white doves they release on that day, in August, isn't it?" You began to talk sadly about the doves that are hired out for the show. I had never even thought about anything like that, I had just assumed they would fly away freely afterwards. "That's what I like about you!" you said, and cooing like the pigeons you pecked at my body using the tip of your nose as a beak.

(Calms down and turns off tape)

It was the day before Christmas Eve. That evening a phone call came from your pâtisserie friend. You were in bed reading, as you said you didn't feel too well. "Oh, that's all right, I think it's a great idea. I'll deliver them for you – your time is too precious at the moment, it's such a busy period…" You hung up, took off your pyjamas, put on a sweater and some trousers and went out with your van. To deliver cakes… cakes for the elderly residents of old people's homes who had no relatives to look after them.

(Sound of a car stopping outside. Hiroko leaves the room as if afraid. The car door closes and it drives on. The room gets slightly darker. A woman wearing light sunglasses and carrying a flower comes in through the half-open door, feeling her way.)

KAZUKO: Where can she be? Leaving the door wide open like that! The shopkeeper next door said she should be in, but…

What a location – it's so shaded by the buildings around that no sunlight comes in, even at midday. Why on earth is she living in a place like this,

I wonder, a solitary room hidden in an urban hollow? It's like a warehouse on some dead planet out in space…

(Smells the flower she is still holding)

"I know you like a flower… a flower without a name"

(Hiroko enters, full of energy. Kazuko hurriedly takes off her sunglasses and puts them into her handbag.)

HIROKO:	Kazuko, hello, do come in! Fancy coming all the way from Haneda to a place like this, when I could have gone to Narita!

KAZUKO:	Hello Hiroko… it's been a while, hasn't it?

HIROKO:	Shall I take your coat?

KAZUKO:	Oh, thank you.

(Hiroko takes coat and runs offstage)

KAZUKO:	Don't rush…

HIROKO:	OK!

(Re-enters)

KAZUKO:	Here you are!

(Hands over flower)

HIROKO:	Thank you!

KAZUKO: How've you been keeping? Oh look! Do you still ride a bicycle, even here?

HIROKO: (*Looking at the flower*) Yes, any time I have something to do nearby…

KAZUKO: Well, you are still young, aren't you!

(*The two speak together*)

KAZUKO: Why don't you recon…?

HIROKO: Why don't you reconsider?

(*Look at each other and smile*)

HIROKO: How long is it for this time?

KAZUKO: Same as always, two weeks…

HIROKO: Are you going to meet up over there?

KAZUKO: With whom?

HIROKO: English Papa.

KAZUKO: Yes. Papa has apparently hurt his leg, so I really do want to pay him a visit while I'm there.

HIROKO: It must be terrible for 'Daddy Long-legs' to injure his leg…

KAZUKO: Ah, you heard that from Tōru, right?

(Hiroko makes no sign of assent or dissent)

KAZUKO: Tōru never liked Papa.

HIROKO: You were the only one who ever mentioned English Papa to me.

(Runs offstage and guides the bar staff as they bring on a table with the flower in a vase, then two chairs)

KAZUKO: *(Recollecting)* I was five, and Tōru had just reached two… Tōru…

HIROKO: He told me, "I can't remember anything, I truly can't, it's simply not there in my memory – and that's what is so upsetting".

(Goes back offstage to bring on a tray with two cups and a teapot)

KAZUKO: So how many months did it last?

HIROKO: Hm?

KAZUKO: You and my brother, Tōru…

HIROKO: Starting from when?

KAZUKO: Well…

HIROKO: Eight months. It was the eighth month.

KAZUKO: Oh Hiroko!

HIROKO: That's when he died… I remember now, you were over in England that time as well.

KAZUKO: Actually that's not so – I was in France, at Nice.

HIROKO: We phoned London time and time again. I got Mum to phone. But she said that nobody answered.

KAZUKO: I hadn't realized that Papa's family always spent the Christmas holidays at their villa in Nice. We had flown to Nice from London just that day, the 23rd of December. The winter in Nice is grey, with a strong wind blowing. There's a small airport on the shore. I had heard that the sea changes colour with the sun, and it was true: in mid-summer the Mediterranean would sparkle all the colours of the rainbow, but under the winter sky the ocean turned grey.

(Hiroko pours tea and sits down stage left)

We drove along the Promenade des Anglais and the curved shore road which leads to Grasse, the perfume town. The road is flanked by huge mansions, and then there it is: Papa's villa, set back a little. There are tall stone pillars at the gate, and an interphone through which you speak to the doorman. Then the iron gates open without a sound, and you drive through into a large forest, on and on. After a while you come to a huge wooden garage, separated into right and left sides, and with enough space for six cars. It was full of limousines, parked haphazardly as though they had been abandoned there. In the drawing room to the right of the porch, we could see the red glow of a wood fire.

Beyond the drawing room there is a garden, with a swimming pool for the summer months. On a small rise, there's a table complete with cooking area – it must have been big enough for a dinner party of around twenty people. Throughout the forest you can see statues by Papa's favourite contemporary sculptors, just scattered about.

If you follow one of the narrow paths into the forest, you arrive at a little glen filled with the noise of a small stream. When you're in the forest, you don't sense the difference between Nice's summer and winter as vividly as you do at the shore.

So I had no kind of premonition whatsoever. As usual, I hadn't even left Tōru any contact details.

HIROKO: That couldn't be helped.

KAZUKO: Couldn't you find out anything more detailed at the hospital?

HIROKO: *(While stirring tea)* Myocardial infarction.

KAZUKO: But if they had done a proper post-mortem…

HIROKO: It would have made no difference. We've talked about this so many times, Kazuko.

KAZUKO: I'm sorry. It's because I wasn't there at the time. But then again, it might have made a difference.

HIROKO: You said yourself, you had no idea anything like that was going to happen.

KAZUKO: True… I was having fun. With English Papa's family, listening to Papa explain my situation… Anna asked "Papa, how did you pick her?" and so he spoke about it, for the first time. "Well, we were in this church hall in Hiroshima, and the names of all the children were

13

listed in a row, like so… I took a dart and threw it at the list, saying I'd adopt whichever one it hit." "Hmm, so that's how you picked her?" "Yes, that's right. Of course, I was still single then…" Anna looked at me quite mischievously. That's because Papa always introduced me to people as his eldest daughter.

HIROKO: What a cruel way to decide, by throwing a dart.

KAZUKO: Not at all, it's more like Cupid's arrow of love! How could anyone choose one child from a mass of orphans? It could be nothing other than fate, a spin of Fortune's wheel. Did you know, Papa had come to England as a refugee himself?

HIROKO: *(Shocked)* No, really?

KAZUKO: Yes – he was Czech. He had fled before the Nazi occupation, seeing as he was of Jewish descent. That evening was the first time I heard that story too… Ever since I was a small child, I had been happy that the person who helped raise me via the moral adoption programme was from England. I didn't want to call anyone from the country that had dropped the atomic bomb 'Papa'. Not the country that had used the bomb which killed our real father.

(Sits down, stage right)

KAZUKO: I still don't know where our real father died.

(Hiroko is silent, as if holding herself back)

KAZUKO: Thinking back, our home must have been near the hypocentre… Mother had taken Tōru and me to Granny's house, for safety. That day, Mother left the house with Tōru before I got up, to take a change of clothes and some food to Father, because he had stayed behind in our own house.

HIROKO: Your mother was holding Tōru in both arms, wasn't she? Because she was carrying everything else in a rucksack?

KAZUKO: Yes, that's right. Mother told Granny time and time again, "I was hugging him, just like this…" Apparently it happened when they were waiting for a tram at Koi station. Mother was chased up Koi hill by the fire – she couldn't go on to Father's place. Granny said that in fact those who fled to high places showed even worse after-effects. After two days we had still had no word, so Granny took me into town to look for Tōru and my parents. What really captivated me was the body of a large horse: it had been burnt as black as charcoal. It's strange in a way, but even now when I try to remember, all I can recollect is the whole town looking light brown.

It was on the tenth that Mother came back to Granny's place and died. There was not a single scar on Mother's body, but blood was pouring out of her nose and mouth, and she was in agony. I was told to take Tōru into the back garden and play. By the time we were called back in, Mother was already dead with a white cloth over her face.

Neither Tōru nor I cried… I can remember how serene and beautiful Mother looked, compared to all the burnt corpses we had seen in the town. I couldn't think of her as being anything other than tired and sleeping.

HIROKO: Tōru couldn't remember any of this.

KAZUKO: *(Standing)* It was decided that I should be raised in my aunt's home. By the time I left it was already the middle of September. The boy next door took a photo of the two of us in a sunflower field.

(Hiroko runs towards back of room and pauses; Kazuko does not notice)

KAZUKO: That photo… Tōru sitting on a chair, and me standing next to him… Tōru said that the sunflowers looked like Mother, protecting us… After that day, my brother and I never lived in the same house.

HIROKO: Kazuko…

KAZUKO: You managed to live together for a whole 80 days…

HIROKO: But the two of you were brother and sister, next of kin!

(Puts hand on Kazuko's shoulder)

KAZUKO: Quite. Husband and wife don't count as blood relations, do they? Maybe because their blood isn't truly linked unless they have a child?

(Hiroko staggers back)

HIROKO: But the two of us had been searching for each other… I've finally understood this now, ten whole years later.

KAZUKO: Yes, that's right – it was because you were called Hiroko. My brother told me.

HIROKO: He wasn't just looking for a girl named 'Hiroko'! It was only after we met that Tōru first asked, "So what do they call you?"

KAZUKO: Have it your own way.

(Kazuko sits; Hiroko disgruntledly goes and switches tape on)

KAZUKO: You weren't even born when that other Hiroko died. She was a high school student, the same year as Tōru.

Just like Tōru, she didn't suffer a single injury on the day the bomb fell, but 15 years later, in 1960, she suddenly died from radiation sickness.

Hiroko was anæmic, and her body lost the ability to absorb frozen blood from the blood bank. She would sometimes get blood donations from the people who came to visit her in hospital.

(Hiroko sits)

KAZUKO: Apparently she used to thank them with a bright smile, saying, "Thank you ever so much. This blood is warm, so it doesn't hurt in the slightest. This is going to help me get well again, isn't it?" Some of her classmates and other children would fold paper cranes and send them to her hospital room, as a prayer that she really would get better. Hiroko used to write letters too, saying, "We mustn't let Pikadon[2] kill us!", yet…

---

[2] *Literally 'flash-bang' – the word first used to describe the atomic bomb by those who had experienced it*

HIROKO: I heard all about it from Tōru. He said that he had wanted to become a doctor from the day that Hiroko died. They were the same age…

"Grown-ups are idiots. Why on earth did they fight the war? Why did they force me to undergo such agony? Why did I have to catch such a terrible disease and suffer this way? All the others died in agony too, didn't they, from the same disease?" Tōru would often talk about Hiroko, clutching her light brown book…

KAZUKO: Ah, so you've read it too? "Notes from the movement to preserve the A-bomb dome", the one with Hiroko's diary in it?

HIROKO: Tōru's precious book – I've got it here. Wait a minute…

(Hiroko goes to next room. Kazuko hurriedly takes some medicine out of her handbag and drops it into her eyes, then puts it back into her bag. Hiroko re-enters holding the book, turns the tape off, and reads)

HIROKO: "At 8:15 on the morning of August 6th, the Peace Bell sounds, and messages from the foreign representatives are read out. Yet the memories of the terrifying atomic bomb that fell 14 years ago at this time on this day are still burning their way into the chests of the people of Hiroshima, even 14 years later – or rather, for a lifetime. If, by the time the next century comes, people should have forgotten it, the words on the memorial stone and the painful image of the Industrial Promotion Hall alone will remain as witnesses, transmitting the terror of the atomic bomb to later generations.

"Beneath this hot August sun, maggots bred in the keloids, causing the victims to writhe in excruciating pain. There must be tens of thousands of people who shared this experience of being a hibakusha, deprived even of the right to family life. These people, taunted for being orphans and unable to convey their distress to those around... if there is any love left in this world, we should look at them with affection and watch over them warmly, as a parent or child would. How else could I look them in the face? What right do I have to be healthy? I too saw the atomic bomb, but at the moment I have no symptoms of illness, and no real cause for concern. Yet it is said that people who saw the bomb die young. When I hear things like that, I think 'well, maybe my time will come tomorrow, maybe even today'.

(Kazuko stands up)

HIROKO: "And once I begin to think like that, I start wanting to do something for the sake of other people, for myself too – but you need money to do anything, and so I'm at a loss for what I can do. If only I had more money, I would be able to do something to help other people, and also myself. It really does seem to be the case that people who have to overcome great hardship turn out to be the strongest, the most pure at heart."

(Kazuko wobbles slightly; it could be seen as the fault of her high-heels. Hiroko moves to support her, but holds back)

HIROKO: Being able to live with one's family seems to have been quite important...

KAZUKO: *(Dabbing at her eyes with a handkerchief)* I was so well treated at my aunt's house... When I was young, she would have shoes specially made for me, while her own children had to wear off the shelf items. For a long, long time she was very careful to ensure that all the money English Papa sent was used only on my behalf... I was just a child, but I still sensed the discrimination. Yet I have never been able to speak about it before – even now, I can only do it because it's you I'm speaking to.

Taking care of someone else's child and bringing them up is not a simple task at all.

HIROKO: You were invited over to England when you were twenty, after your Coming of Age ceremony, weren't you?

KAZUKO: That's right. It was the year Hiroko died. I travelled to English Papa's place by ship. Papa was a banker, and he sent a Rolls-Royce to pick me up from the port at Southampton. He had also already gone through all the procedures to get me signed up for an English course at Oxford, to help me study the language and get used to the British way of life. That was the first time I met Papa.

HIROKO: But you'd been writing to each other for ages, hadn't you?

KAZUKO: You bet! *(Sits)* As you know, the pastor of Nagarekawa Church held sessions every Saturday for children who had been 'morally adopted'…

(Hiroko sits)

KAZUKO: How I looked forward to them! To be able to have someone write down what I was thinking and send it off to my English Papa… I was too young to read English then, so I have no idea how the letters actually turned out, but I dreamed such fantastic things! Every Saturday I would head off with a letter, and I couldn't wait for the next weekend to come. As they say, absence makes the heart grow fonder.

HIROKO: Uh-huh…

KAZUKO: At that age, a single letter would keep me happy for at least a month!

HIROKO: So you were in a world of your own, weren't you? Tōru was left by himself…

KAZUKO: That's not true! It's not true at all! I was always thinking of Tōru. Even when I went to England, I was constantly trying to think of a way I might be able to bring Tōru across, to English Papa's place – but overcoming the language barrier was not so easy.

HIROKO: Tōru used to say: "Throughout my life, I've avoided relying on other people too much…"

KAZUKO: Ha! That just shows how little he knew about the toil Granny was putting in… and how much he had to go through himself. Granny claimed benefits all the time he was at high school, and some local people complained to the district welfare commissioner, who told her, "You've got a grandson haven't you? Get him to work for you!" But Granny was tough, and answered defiantly, "You expect me to cause yet more hardship to my grandson? If so, then give us back the ones who died in the atomic bomb! Give him back his parents, and give me back my son!"

HIROKO: Ohh…

KAZUKO: Tōru started to become more independent and support himself by means of some part-time work once he'd left home to attend a veterinary college in Tokyo. So I suppose it is true that I never gave Tōru any real assistance… in fact, I always paid more attention to my cousins, with whom I'd been brought up. Well I mean, my aunt had raised me without anybody's assistance or guarantees: all the funds that came from the moral adoption programme went for me alone, and she never received any reward for herself or the rest of her family…

HIROKO: I'm sorry, Kazuko, shooting my mouth off about something I don't really know anything about…

KAZUKO: Hiroko, that's not what I'm saying! It must have sounded as though I were blaming you, but I'm reproaching myself. Forgive me. My aunt is growing old, and that's why I feel an urge to say thank-you – to shout it out loud – to my aunt and all the many other people who brought up A-bomb orphans. I wish I could do something for them in return! That's at the forefront of my mind, and so my mouth ran away with me… I do apologize. Sometimes I feel I need to apologize to Tōru too.

HIROKO: Oh Kazuko…

KAZUKO: And the fact that you only told me about your marriage at the same time as all your other friends… I kept griping about that, too.

HIROKO: I feel bad about that…

KAZUKO: You must have found your new sister-in-law so irritating. Perhaps Tōru did too. Being single for such a long time… The reason I am still single is that I was more realistic than my brother. I was afraid to get married, have children, and then leave them as orphans like us. Would I still be alive when the children came of age…? That was what worried me.

And then, despite having got married, Tōru went and died before me…

HIROKO: It was a real shock when I received a note from the town hall, the year after Tōru died, to say that his name would be added to the list of those who had died as a result of the atomic bomb, and placed inside the memorial sarcophagus on August 6th. So many years since that day, and there's me suddenly a bomb widow at 21…!

KAZUKO: Hiroko!

HIROKO: *(Stands up)* I left the city that autumn. Tōru had been nursing his grandmother and only married me after she had died, so there was nothing left to do in that city… *(Trying not to cry)* No, that's a lie! There was everything left to do. Tōru had left it all behind for me. Everything the other Hiroko had wanted to do… everything Tōru had wanted to do … That's how I see it now, sometimes… But it's not that easy, you know!

KAZUKO: Hiroko, you must have been so lonely these ten years…

HIROKO: Lonely… ? Far from it. Tōru was always by my side… The reason I chose this location for 'Le Soleil' is that he liked rivers at night-time. Ten years ago we attended our first – and as it turned out, our last – August 6th Tōrō-nagashi. He wrote the names of his dead father and mother on the lantern and floated it down the river. So when I stand by a river in the dark, it's like being together with him again…

(Laughs hysterically, crying) Rubbish! What rubbish! He told me once: "Lies and deception are not permitted to those who do medicine… even though there are occasions when you do have to lie. But the medical profession does not suit people like me, who spend their whole lives deceiving themselves."

KAZUKO: Tōru was no liar…

HIROKO: He was too honest for his own good! He did not have the strength to look at himself openly, and that scared him… Did you know, Tōru had never been for a check-up?

(Kazuko is stunned, lost for words)

HIROKO: That day, after he had finished delivering the cakes to the pensioners' homes, he left his van in front of the house, went back to bed, and watched the TV news. I was rather surprised, as I was expecting him to tell me how much the old people had rejoiced, what the mood had been like, and so on… Then all of a sudden he rushed into the toilet, and vomited. "That's odd," I thought, "he hasn't eaten that much". Then he went to throw up again. The third time, I went up to the toilet door and asked, "Are you OK?" He replied, "Hiroko, I can't see a thing! Phone a doctor, immediately!" I helped him back to bed, laid him down, and called our family doctor.

The doctor asked the nurse accompanying him to call for an ambulance. I didn't know what to think. Tōru was put on an intravenous drip, but three hospitals refused to admit him. By the time we arrived at a hospital with a heart surgery department, the monitor was showing cardiac arrest, but they tried massaging the heart and other such treatments, and the ECG started up again. The nurse told me that he had regained consciousness and was calling my name, and urged me to go in. I went into the operating theatre, and…

(Kazuko sobs; hearing the voice, Hiroko regains her calm)

HIROKO: Kazuko, I'm so sorry, bringing this up again…

KAZUKO: No, on the contrary, it's my fault, I never intended today…

HIROKO: He was worried for you. Because you are really a secondary radiation victim, considering the long time you spent in the city searching for your father…

KAZUKO: Medically speaking, that's true. But Granny said not to apply for the Hibakusha Certificate, as it would ruin my marriage prospects, so she didn't let my aunt go through the relevant procedures.

HIROKO: But surely you could still do it now?

KAZUKO: The number of applicants has been increasing recently, so they now request witnesses. And the procedures have apparently become more difficult. But anyway, I don't want to become a burden on society now – I've been privileged with a good life so far…

HIROKO: In that case, why do you keep asking about his post-mortem?

KAZUKO: Because he was a hibakusha…

HIROKO: Because he was a direct hibakusha?

KAZUKO: Yes of course. Surely it's possible that Tōru suffered from anæmia, and this put a load upon his heart?

HIROKO: Well, he was in any case plump enough for some people to suggest he lose weight…

KAZUKO: Tōru did enjoy his food…

HIROKO: He was such a kind man, so good-hearted. Once we ate some snails in their shells, the French way – what are they called? – escargots. I had never even seen them before, and he casually explained the easiest way to eat them, demonstrating first himself, so that I could relax and really enjoy the meal. He was somehow able to sense what people were thinking.

KAZUKO: Even though he had never been abroad…

HIROKO: Apparently he learned how to eat them from the woman running the pâtisserie – she was French herself, you see.

KAZUKO: Oh really?

(Hiroko switches on the light at the back of the stage, which suddenly becomes very bright. Kazuko is startled and flinches for an instant, instinctively shielding her eyes. Hiroko does not notice.)

KAZUKO: Ah!

(The walls are covered in black and white photos of sunflowers, arranged like wallpaper. Some simple tables and chairs are tidied away at the side.)

HIROKO: This furniture was all hand-made by Tōru. He had placed it in some of the restaurants in Hiroshima, but I managed to persuade them to return it to me. It is all work from the period when your grandmother was still in good health, so he didn't just design them but actually made them all with his own hands.

(Kazuko wanders across and touches the furniture)

KAZUKO: Tōru never let anyone into his workshop, so…

HIROKO: I got him to take me to the restaurants where these tables
and chairs were being used several times! That's how I managed to persuade them later…

(Puts on tape of music – tango)

He was a good dancer, too…

(Picks up a chair and dances with it)

Tōru's handiwork! He often said that he would like to design me by
hand too…

(Kazuko approaches the wall and looks fixedly at the sunflowers)

KAZUKO: These photos, where are they from?

HIROKO: Tōru.

KAZUKO: What?!

HIROKO: That one photo where the two of you are pictured together… It was Tōru's treasure, a precious record of the day he had no
memory of. That's why he kept on taking these photos, year after year,
every summer. He'd be quite bashful when he showed them to me, saying, "They're only amateur snapshots, you know…". He took so many!

KAZUKO: *(Crying)* Tōru!

(Hiroko stops dancing)

HIROKO: Tōru taught me so many things, but for ten years now, I
haven't been able to do any of them. He used to go to that memorial

stone in Peace Park on the 6th of every month and clean it. He told me he had done that ever since he graduated and returned to Hiroshima from Tokyo. *(Suddenly changes tone)* Kazuko, that day in the operating theatre, when he called my name… what do you think he said?

(Kazuko simply shakes her head)

HIROKO: He spoke directly into my ear, *(shouting)* "Take care of Kazuko for me… Her songs!"

(Kazuko staggers back. Hiroko collapses and crawls around, then climbs to her feet again.)

HIROKO: My legs just gave way. His eyes were wide open, as though the lids had been ripped off. It was all over.

I just crawled around the floor screaming. I wasn't crying. It was more like a guttural moan, produced from the innermost core of my body, thrusting its way out, unstoppable. The nurse and doctor left me alone for a while. Yes, I was simply crawling around…

KAZUKO: Hiroko!

HIROKO: I didn't go near his body after that.

(Stops the tape)

The crematorium schedule meant that we couldn't wait for you to return to Japan.

KAZUKO: I'm sorry. *(Shouts)* But why… my brother's last words… why did you never tell me until now?

HIROKO: How could I tell you? I had no idea how you would react, if I had told you just after you came back from England…

But maybe it was rather resentment. I felt such a grudge against you. At the time I thought you were more important to him than I was…

But over these ten years, I've gradually begun to understand. I really felt like telling you on the second anniversary of his death. But I didn't. I didn't want you to think that I was remaining single because of his last words… And now, I've at long last understood. He saw me as being one half of himself, and as such, I had to make sure that Kazuko was all right – to ensure your happiness…

KAZUKO: My happiness…

HIROKO: Kazuko, you should free yourself, and do more of what you truly enjoy… It is really songs you like, isn't it?

KAZUKO: Of course I love singing… But I am free.

HIROKO: You really think so? You spend all your time helping your aunt. Just like Tōru did – staying single until there was no longer a need to care for his grandmother…

KAZUKO: That's not really true – after all, I get to go abroad several times a year… Recently our customers have become more choosy: they don't merely go for the big brands any more. In haute couture, they've become very selective about the fabrics they want, and my work now tends to consist of seeking them out. Silk has to be from Italy, and so on, you know… For jewellery too, they want antique items fitted to ready-made dresses, so that they can go to parties wearing something no one else in Japan has. That's the current trend. So sometimes I consult your mother too… There's still so much to be done. I do enjoy running the shop with my aunt.

HIROKO: And today's trip is for the same purpose, right?

KAZUKO: That's right. Just look at me! I'm totally free, working quite how I please, and enjoying every minute. As for the songs… well, now I sing for myself, that's all that's changed. Nobody else could understand, no one else has been through the same experience…

HIROKO: What about men, Kazuko, have you never fallen in love?

KAZUKO: *(Laughing)* Of course I have, several times. But it's just like selecting a fabric…

(Caresses the flower)

I like attractive things, and with men as well, I prefer handsome ones… *(last words like a song)*

HIROKO: I'm serious!

KAZUKO: *(Sings)*

> "I know you like a flower
> A flower without a name
> I'd like them all to see you
> But you are so far away
> All I have's your memory…"

(Hiroko claps)

KAZUKO: *(laughs)* I'm sorry, my voice is awful!

(Looks at her watch)

Oh, Hiroko, is it already this late? I'm afraid I must be going…

HIROKO: Do you have to?

(Kazuko takes her sunglasses out of her bag)

KAZUKO: Hiroko, thank you. I really mean it. You told me Tōru's last words at just the right time…

 (Starts to put sunglasses on)

HIROKO: Kazuko, is something wrong with your eyes?

KAZUKO: No no, nothing.

(Replaces the glasses in the handbag)

Nobody would understand, would they?

HIROKO: Understand what?

KAZUKO: About the two of us…

HIROKO: The two…?

KAZUKO: Yes, me and you…

HIROKO: Well as for me, I am the owner of "Le Soleil"

KAZUKO: And me a globe-hopper?

HIROKO: Ah, your coat! *(Runs and fetches it)* Here you are, you don't want to be late…

KAZUKO: When are you going to come to Hiroshima?

HIROKO: Sometime soon…

KAZUKO: It would be nice if you could make it two weeks from now…

HIROKO: *(Playfully)* Of course, I do have engagements of my own to work around…

KAZUKO: It's the first time for us, isn't it, arranging a next meeting?

HIROKO: OK, so let's take a souvenir photograph. Over there!

(Hurriedly fetches camera, and sets up the automatic shutter. Gestures to Kazuko to stand by Tōru's hand-made table, in front of the sunflower photos)

Right then, you stand there, and I'll sit on the chair…

KAZUKO: Just like Tōru…

(Noise of shutter)

KAZUKO: OK then…

HIROKO: Give my love to 'Daddy Long-legs' when you get to London!

KAZUKO: Aah, Tōru often said the same thing…

HIROKO: See you!

KAZUKO: Bye-bye!

(Hiroko sees Kazuko out. The phone rings.)

HIROKO: Hello? Oh, hello Mum! So how about it? Ridiculous? Come on, don't you think it's a great idea? "Le Soleil" is doing fine here, so… I really want to do it, set up a restaurant & bar on a boat in Hiroshima Bay. Oh yes, that's not a bad idea either! We could use the cabins as a posh hotel most of the time, but then in August change it into a free hostel. You know, for all the young foreigners who come for the 6th. Oh but look, there are so many of them, all sleeping out. It's a great plan!

And seeing as it only takes an hour to fly there from Tokyo, I could even stay in Hiroshima a few weeks myself! Guess what Mum, I've decided to listen to your advice from now on, so… Oh yes, Kazuko was just, yes that's right, Tōru's sister Kazuko. From Narita airport… Has she already asked you about these antique brooches? It's a while since I last saw her, but she looked great. Yes, well I should be back in around a fortnight, so start asking around your top contacts – get some tips on how that kind of business is run, OK? Right! Thanks Mum, bye!

(Hangs up, and switches off light at back of stage. While stretching…)

Ten years… well, my sunflowers, it looks like the sun might have come up again.

(Slight pause. As if murmuring to herself)

Yellow was the Jews' badge of death
Sunflowers… Van Gogh died too
But Papa's dart was the arrow of Cupid
Sunflowers, embracing the sunlight…
I feel I may be able to go back there…
Even though until just a minute ago, until meeting Kazuko, I
had lost touch with where I was, what I was doing.

*(Fade out. Suddenly a blinding flash of lightning, a clap of thunder, and
the noise of rain beating down)*

✿ ✿ ✿

Epilogue

Two women. Kazuko appears in a black dress wearing sunglasses, then
Hiroko appears in a white dress… Gives Kazuko her cheek as if sup-
porting and consoling her… The two dance the tango together.

Then the sunglasses fly off, Kazuko shields her eyes with her hand, and
Hiroko moves away and watches over her. Two spotlights circle each
other on stage, gradually merging into one circle, in whose light Kazuko
crumples to the floor.